Emeraldalicious

WRITTEN AND ILLUSTRATED
BY Victoria Kann

SCHOLASTIC INC.

THANK

ISBN 978-0-545-73787-6

Copyright © 2013 by Victoria Kann. All rights reserved. Published by Scholastic Inc.,
557 Broadway, New York, NY 10012, by arrangement with HarperCollins Children's Books, a division of
HarperCollins Publishers. PINKALICIOUS and all related logos and characters are trademarks of Victoria Kann.
Used with permission. Based on the HarperCollins book *Pinkalicious* written by Victoria Kann and
Elizabeth Kann, illustrated by Victoria Kann. SCHOLASTIC and associated logos are
trademarks and/or registered trademarks of Scholastic Inc.

12 11 10 9 8 7 6 5 4 3 2 1   14 15 16 17 18 19/0

Printed in the U.S.A.   40

First Scholastic printing, April 2014

The artist used mixed media to create the
digital illustrations for this book.
Typography by Rachel Zegar

I was strolling in the park with my brother, Peter.

Suddenly I tripped on a rock and fell, breaking my tiara and wand.

"Oh no! Look at your wand! You never go anywhere without it," said Peter. "What are you going to do?"

"I have an idea! I'll make a new one out of this stick," I said.

"And you can use these vines," said Peter.
"And that flower!" I said, pointing to a plant
I had never seen before.

"I love you, pretty wand!" I said, kissing the wand.

The wand began to sparkle.

"Wow! Did you see that?" said Peter.

"Are you a MAGIC wand?" I asked, and the wand flew out of my hand.

"Come back here!" I yelled. The wand did not listen to me.

"I am Pinkalicious, the Princess of Pink, and I command you to return to me!"

The wand paused, and then flew farther up the path.

"Maybe it isn't listening to you because you don't have a crown or a cape like a real princess," said Peter.

"You're right!" I said. I picked some flowers and made a crown. Then I tied leaves together and wove flowers to make a cape.

"I am the Princess of Flowers!" I announced.

When we turned the corner, I found the magic wand on a pile of garbage.

"Yuck!" said Peter. "It smells."

I reached for the wand, but it flew up into a tree.

"What a sad tree! Its leaves are dropping." I climbed the tree and grabbed my magic wand.

"This is where we had picnics! What happened?" asked Peter.

"This used to be my favorite park," I said.

Suddenly there was a loud crack. The tree swayed,
and the branch that I was sitting on broke.
I fell to the ground with a thud.
"OUCH!"

"Harrumph! I need a chair."
I waved the magic wand and said,

"Buckets, bow tie, and a bone.
All this garbage makes me groan.
What I would love is a pretty throne."

Garbage started flying through the sky and then magically
transformed into a throne.

"Did that REALLY happen?" I gasped.
"Wow! You should make a castle!" said Peter.
"Make a castle!" I commanded.
Nothing happened.

"What a silly wand!" I said, and threw it to the ground.
The wand sparkled.
"It has to work, since it worked before and made the throne!"
insisted Peter.
"Hmm, what did I say when I made the throne?" I asked Peter.

Peter giggled, imitating me in a high-pitched voice—
"You said, 'What I would love . . .'"
"Look, Peter! When you said 'love,' a little flower bloomed!
Love," I whispered. Another flower opened.
"Love," I said again, and a third flower blossomed.

"Suitcase, snorkel, stinky shoe.
I love pink, purple, and blue.
Make me flowers in every hue!"

I waved my magic wand, and flowers grew out of the ground.

"HEY, HOW DID YOU DO THAT?" asked Peter.

"It's easy! Take the wand, describe what is around you, and ask for what you want with love. . . ."

"And make up a rhyme!" added Peter.

"Watch me," I said.

"Grapefruit, girdle, and a glove.
Make a place filled with love.
Bring in birds from up above!"

Garbage started flying in a million directions, and colorful, twittering birds appeared.

"Let me try!" Peter begged, and quickly said,

"Television, towel, and a tassel.
I'm a prince who loves his castle.
Please make me one without a hassle!"

A castle appeared.
"IT WORKS! Look, it even has a moat! It took the garbage and made a castle! I can't believe it!" said Peter.
"Wow! What else can we make?"

"I know . . ." I said.

"Telephone, teacup, and twine.
I'd love a dress that's really fine.
Take this trash and make it mine!"

Right before my eyes, a beautiful new outfit was made.

"Now I'll make something for you, Peter.

"Hairbrush, hanger, harp, and heel.
What I love is this old wheel. . . ." I said.

"Recycle it into a boat mobile!" finished Peter.

"Let me do it. This is fun!" Peter said, grabbing the wand.
"I want to make a cookie-candy-cupcake-ice-cream machine that makes a different flavor of sweets every ten minutes, and a robot to clean my room, and then a great big rocket!"

"Peter, come back here NOW! I'll share with you, but it's MY turn, and I have a really good wish!"

"Let's fix this garbage dump," I said. "It sure is ugly and stinky!

"Detergent, doughnut, and dirty dishes.
Pinkalicious loves her wishes.
Make this place Emeraldalicious!"

I waved my magic wand . . .
. . . and the dump transformed
into a greenatastic garden.

Just then, there was a gust of wind. The magic wand broke apart and filled the sky with sparkly seeds.

"OH NO! What are we going to do without the wand? We can't make things happen anymore." Peter cried, "The magic is gone!"

"Don't worry, Peter. We still have everything we need!" I said. "We have these seeds, and with a little love we can make the entire world EMERALDALICIOUS!"

"And that would be greenerrific!" said Peter.